PACKERS™

Go, Pack, Go!

Aimee Aryal

Illustrated by Miguel De Angel

MASCOT
BOOKS®
www.mascotbooks.com

It was a beautiful fall day in Green Bay, Wisconsin. Packers fans from all over the Badger State were on their way to historic Lambeau Field to watch their beloved Green Bay Packers play football.

All over town, everyone dressed in Packers green and gold. As fans made their way to the stadium, they cheered, "Go, Pack, Go!"

Hours before the start of the game, Packers fans began gathering in the parking lot. The smell of good food was in the air as smoke billowed from grills. Some children, and even a few grown-ups, painted their faces for the game!

As fans walked through
the Lambeau Field gates, they
cheered, "Go, Pack, Go!"

The team gathered in the locker room before the game. Players strapped on their pads and dressed in their classic Green Bay Packers uniforms. Wearing the Packers green and gold made each player feel proud to be a part of the team's championship tradition.

The coach delivered final instructions and encouraged the team to play their best. The coach cheered, "Go, Pack, Go!"

It was now time for the Green Bay Packers to take the field. The announcer called, "Ladies and gentlemen, please welcome your Green Bay Packers!" The Packers sprinted onto the field and were greeted by their loyal fans. It was very loud in the stadium!

The Packers huddled around the team captains and cheered, "Go, Pack, Go!"

The team captains met at midfield for the coin toss. The referee flipped a coin high in the air and the visiting team called, "Heads." The coin landed with the heads side up – the Packers would begin the game by kicking off.

The referee reminded the players that it was important to play hard, but also with good sportsmanship.

The Packers kicker booted the ball down the field to start the action. With the game underway, the kicker cheered, "Go, Pack, Go!"

After the opening kickoff, it was time for the Packers defense to take the field. One fan led the crowd in a "DE-FENSE" chant, holding up a "D" in one hand and a picket fence in the other. With the crowd's encouragement, the Packers defense sacked the quarterback. Fans appreciated the great play and cheered, "Go, Pack, Go!"

After the defense did its job, the Packers offense went to work. With great teamwork, the offense marched down the field. On fourth down, the team was only one yard away from the end zone.

"Let's go for it!" instructed the coach, and the quarterback called a play in the huddle.

The quarterback yelled, "Down. Set. Hike!" before handing the ball to the running back, who crossed the goal line.

TOUCHDOWN!

As the Packers player performed a "Lambeau Leap," the crowd erupted with joy and fans cheered, "Go, Pack, Go!"

At the end of the first half, the Packers headed back to the locker room. The coach stopped to answer a few questions from a television reporter. In the locker room, the team rested and prepared for the second half.

Meanwhile, Packers fans stretched their legs and picked up a few snacks at the concession stands. In the concourse, Packers fans cheered, "Go, Pack, Go!"

In the second half, the temperature dropped and snow began to fall, turning the field into a "Frozen Tundra." The team played hard through the blizzard. Young fans drank hot chocolate to help them stay warm. One little fan was surprised to see herself on the big screen. With everybody watching, she cheered, "Go, Pack, Go!"

With only a few seconds remaining, the score was tied. The Packers lined-up for a field goal try. After a good snap and a perfect hold, the kicker booted the ball toward the goal posts. The stadium was nearly silent as all eyes followed the flight of the ball.

The kick was good!

The Green Bay Packers won the football game! The kicker cheered, "Go, Pack, Go!"

To celebrate the thrilling victory, Packers players dumped water on the coach. The teams shook hands and congratulated each other on a good game. As Packers fans left Lambeau Field, they cheered, "Go, Pack, Go!"

For Anna and Maya. ~ Aimee Aryal

For Sue, Ana Milagros, and Angel Miguel. ~ Miguel De Angel

Green Bay Packers Foundation
The Green Bay Packers Foundation focuses on giving back to the community through a variety of programs that benefit education, civic affairs, health services, human services and youth-related programs. For more information or to donate, contact:

Green Bay Packers Foundation
P.O. Box 10628
Green Bay, WI 54307-0628

Junior Power Pack
Join the official Green Bay Packers kids club, the Junior Power Pack! For more information, call 920-569-7247 or go online to www.packers.com.

For more information, please contact Mascot Books,
P.O. Box 220157, Chantilly, VA 20153-0157

PACKERS, GREEN BAY PACKERS, the OVAL G LOGO, POWER PACK,
and the POWER PACK LOGO, are trademarks or registered trademarks
of The Geen Bay Packers.

ISBN: 978-1-932888-94-2

Printed in the United States.

www.mascotbooks.com

Title List

Baseball

Boston Red Sox	Hello, Wally!	Jerry Remy
Boston Red Sox	Wally The Green Monster And His Journey Through Red Sox Nation!	Jerry Remy
Boston Red Sox	Coast to Coast with Wally The Green Monster	Jerry Remy
Boston Red Sox	A Season with Wally The Green Monster	Jerry Remy
Colorado Rockies	Hello, Dinger!	Aimee Aryal
Detroit Tigers	Hello, Paws!	Aimee Aryal
New York Yankees	Let's Go, Yankees!	Yogi Berra
New York Yankees	Yankees Town	Aimee Aryal
New York Mets	Hello, Mr. Met!	Rusty Staub
New York Mets	Mr. Met and his Journey Through the Big Apple	Aimee Aryal
St. Louis Cardinals	Hello, Fredbird!	Ozzie Smith
Philadelphia Phillies	Hello, Phillie Phanatic!	Aimee Aryal
Chicago Cubs	Let's Go, Cubs!	Aimee Aryal
Chicago White Sox	Let's Go, White Sox!	Aimee Aryal
Cleveland Indians	Hello, Slider!	Bob Feller
Seattle Mariners	Hello, Mariner Moose!	Aimee Aryal
Washington Nationals	Hello, Screech!	Aimee Aryal
Milwaukee Brewers	Hello, Bernie Brewer!	Aimee Aryal

College

Alabama	Hello, Big Al!	Aimee Aryal
Alabama	Roll Tide!	Ken Stabler
Alabama	Big Al's Journey Through the Yellowhammer State	Aimee Aryal
Arizona	Hello, Wilbur!	Lute Olson
Arkansas	Hello, Big Red!	Aimee Aryal
Arkansas	Big Red's Journey Through the Razorback State	Aimee Aryal
Auburn	Hello, Aubie!	Aimee Aryal
Auburn	War Eagle!	Pat Dye
Auburn	Aubie's Journey Through the Yellowhammer State	Aimee Aryal
Boston College	Hello, Baldwin!	Aimee Aryal
Brigham Young	Hello, Cosmo!	LaVell Edwards
Cal - Berkeley	Hello, Oski!	Aimee Aryal
Clemson	Hello, Tiger!	Aimee Aryal
Clemson	Tiger's Journey Through the Palmetto State	Aimee Aryal
Colorado	Hello, Ralphie!	Aimee Aryal
Connecticut	Hello, Jonathan!	Aimee Aryal
Duke	Hello, Blue Devil!	Aimee Aryal
Florida	Hello, Albert!	Aimee Aryal
Florida	Albert's Journey Through the Sunshine State	Aimee Aryal
Florida State	Let's Go, 'Noles!	Aimee Aryal
Georgia	Hello, Hairy Dawg!	Aimee Aryal
Georgia	How 'Bout Them Dawgs!	Vince Dooley
Georgia	Hairy Dawg's Journey Through the Peach State	Vince Dooley
Georgia Tech	Hello, Buzz!	Aimee Aryal
Gonzaga	Spike, The Gonzaga Bulldog	Mike Pringle
Illinois	Let's Go, Illini!	Aimee Aryal
Indiana	Let's Go, Hoosiers!	Aimee Aryal
Iowa	Hello, Herky!	Aimee Aryal
Iowa State	Hello, Cy!	Amy DeLashmutt
James Madison	Hello, Duke Dog!	Aimee Aryal
Kansas	Hello, Big Jay!	Aimee Aryal
Kansas State	Hello, Willie!	Dan Walter
Kentucky	Hello, Wildcat!	Aimee Aryal
LSU	Hello, Mike!	Aimee Aryal
LSU	Mike's Journey Through the Bayou State	Aimee Aryal
Maryland	Hello, Testudo!	Aimee Aryal
Michigan	Let's Go, Blue!	Aimee Aryal
Michigan State	Hello, Sparty!	Aimee Aryal
Minnesota	Hello, Goldy!	Aimee Aryal
Mississippi	Hello, Colonel Rebel!	Aimee Aryal

Pro Football

Carolina Panthers	Let's Go, Panthers!	Aimee Aryal
Chicago Bears	Let's Go, Bears!	Aimee Aryal
Dallas Cowboys	How 'Bout Them Cowboys!	Aimee Aryal
Green Bay Packers	Go, Pack, Go!	Aimee Aryal
Kansas City Chiefs	Let's Go, Chiefs!	Aimee Aryal
Minnesota Vikings	Let's Go, Vikings!	Aimee Aryal
New York Giants	Let's Go, Giants!	Aimee Aryal
New York Jets	J-E-T-S! Jets, Jets, Jets!	Aimee Aryal
New England Patriots	Let's Go, Patriots!	Aimee Aryal
Seattle Seahawks	Let's Go, Seahawks!	Aimee Aryal
Washington Redskins	Hail To The Redskins!	Aimee Aryal

Basketball

Dallas Mavericks	Let's Go, Mavs!	Mark Cuban
Boston Celtics	Let's Go, Celtics!	Aimee Aryal

Other

Kentucky Derby	White Diamond Runs For The Roses	Aimee Aryal
Marine Corps Marathon	Run, Miles, Run!	Aimee Aryal
Mississippi State	Hello, Bully!	Aimee Aryal
Missouri	Hello, Truman!	Todd Donoho
Nebraska	Hello, Herbie Husker!	Aimee Aryal
North Carolina	Hello, Rameses!	Aimee Aryal
North Carolina	Rameses' Journey Through the Tar Heel State	Aimee Aryal
North Carolina St.	Hello, Mr. Wuf!	Aimee Aryal
North Carolina St.	Mr. Wuf's Journey Through North Carolina	Aimee Aryal
Notre Dame	Let's Go, Irish!	Aimee Aryal
Ohio State	Hello, Brutus!	Aimee Aryal
Ohio State	Brutus' Journey	Aimee Aryal
Oklahoma	Let's Go, Sooners!	Aimee Aryal
Oklahoma State	Hello, Pistol Pete!	Aimee Aryal
Oregon	Go Ducks!	Aimee Aryal
Oregon State	Hello, Benny the Beaver!	Aimee Aryal
Penn State	Hello, Nittany Lion!	Aimee Aryal
Penn State	We Are Penn State!	Joe Paterno
Purdue	Hello, Purdue Pete!	Aimee Aryal
Rutgers	Hello, Scarlet Knight!	Aimee Aryal
South Carolina	Hello, Cocky!	Aimee Aryal
South Carolina	Cocky's Journey Through the Palmetto State	Aimee Aryal
So. California	Hello, Tommy Trojan!	Aimee Aryal
Syracuse	Hello, Otto!	Aimee Aryal
Tennessee	Hello, Smokey!	Aimee Aryal
Tennessee	Smokey's Journey Through the Volunteer State	Aimee Aryal
Texas	Hello, Hook 'Em!	Aimee Aryal
Texas	Hook 'Em's Journey Through the Lone Star State	Aimee Aryal
Texas A & M	Howdy, Reveille!	Aimee Aryal
Texas A & M	Reveille's Journey Through the Lone Star State	Aimee Aryal
Texas Tech	Hello, Masked Rider!	Aimee Aryal
UCLA	Hello, Joe Bruin!	Aimee Aryal
Virginia	Hello, CavMan!	Aimee Aryal
Virginia Tech	Hello, Hokie Bird!	Aimee Aryal
Virginia Tech	Yea, It's Hokie Game Day!	Frank Beamer
Virginia Tech	Hokie Bird's Journey Through Virginia	Aimee Aryal
Wake Forest	Hello, Demon Deacon!	Aimee Aryal
Washington	Hello, Harry the Husky!	Aimee Aryal
Washington State	Hello, Butch!	Aimee Aryal
West Virginia	Hello, Mountaineer!	Aimee Aryal
Wisconsin	Hello, Bucky!	Aimee Aryal
Wisconsin	Bucky's Journey Through the Badger State	Aimee Aryal

Order online at **mascotbooks.com** using promo code " **free**" to receive **FREE SHIPPING**!

More great titles coming soon!

info@mascotbooks.com

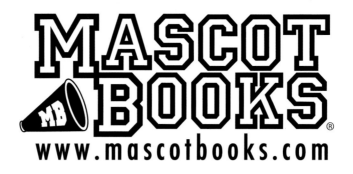
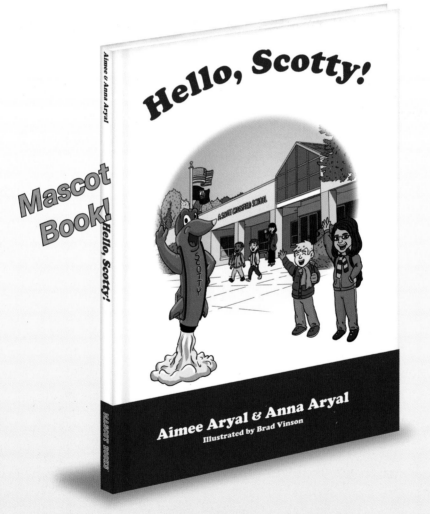